Hallow

Lori Dittmer

CREATIVE EDUCATION • CREATIVE PAPERBACKS

seedlings

Published by Creative Education and Creative Paperbacks
P.O. Box 227, Mankato, Minnesota 56002
Creative Education and Creative Paperbacks
are imprints of The Creative Company
www.thecreativecompany.us

Design by Ellen Huber; production by Colin O'Dea
Art direction by Rita Marshall
Printed in China

Photographs by Alamy (Radharc Images), Getty Images
(Zsuzsanna Mcloughlin/EyeEm, MediaNews Group/
Boulder Daily Camera via Getty Images, Sergeeva/E+),
iStockphoto (4421010037, bondarillia, Noemi Braña,
D-Keine, DenisTangneyJr, GlobalP, jenifoto, mg7,
monkeybusinessimages, nelik, PhotographyFirm, Povareshka,
ryasick, SolStock, welcomia, yukihipo), Shutterstock
(FamVeld)

Library of Congress Cataloging-in-Publication Data
Names: Dittmer, Lori, author.
Title: Halloween / Lori Dittmer.
Series: Seedlings.
Includes index.
Summary: A kindergarten-level introduction to Halloween,
covering the holiday's history, popular traditions, and such
defining symbols as witches and jack-o'-lanterns.
Identifiers: LCCN 2019053293 / ISBN 978-1-64026-329-1
(hardcover) / ISBN 978-1-62832-861-5 (pbk) / ISBN 978-1-
64000-459-7 (eBook)
Subjects: LCSH: Halloween—Juvenile literature.
Classification: LCC GT4965.D57 2020 / DDC 394.261—dc23

CCSS: RI.K.1, 2, 3, 4, 5, 6, 7;
RI.1.1, 2, 3, 4, 5, 6, 7; RF.K.1, 3; RF.1.1

First Edition HC 9 8 7 6 5 4 3 2 1
First Edition PBK 9 8 7 6 5 4 3 2 1

TABLE OF CONTENTS

Hello, Halloween!

Halloween is a day for candy and costumes.

It happens on October 31.

Black cats and witches make people think of Halloween.

Jack-o'-lanterns sit on doorsteps. Black and orange are Halloween colors.

Long ago, people in Europe marked the end of summer.

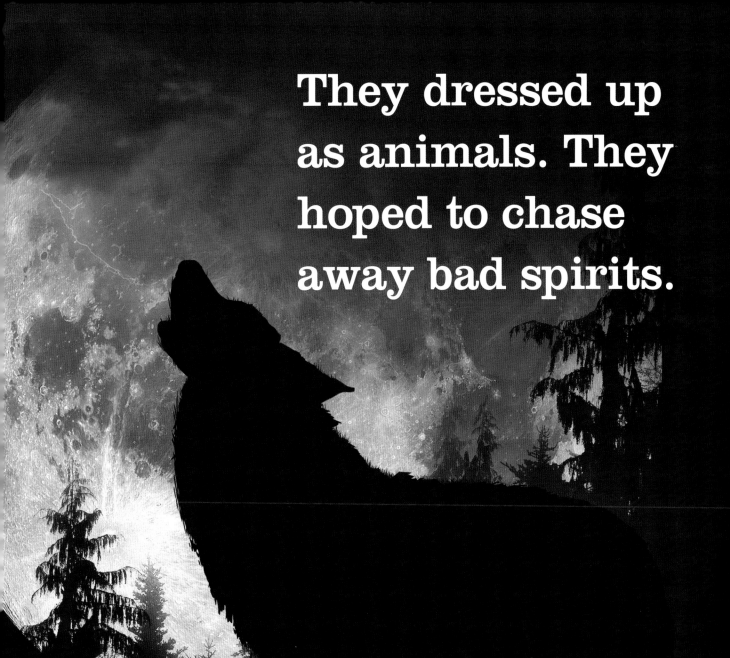

They dressed up as animals. They hoped to chase away bad spirits.

The day was called All Hallows' Eve. People cut holes in turnips. They put lights inside.

Today, children dress up.

They say, "Trick or treat!" They get lots of candy!

People bob for apples.

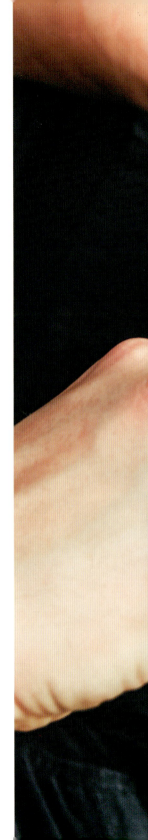

They cut shapes
into pumpkins.

Goodbye, Halloween!

jack-o'-lanterns

black cat

mask

candy

Words to Know

costumes: clothes worn to dress like another person or thing

jack-o'-lanterns: pumpkins that are carved with faces and have lights inside

turnips: rounded vegetables that grow underground

Read More

Grack, Rachel. *Halloween.*
Minneapolis: Bellwether Media, 2017.

Lewis, J. Patrick. *Let's Celebrate Halloween.*
New York: Children's Press, 2018.

Websites

DKfindout: Halloween
https://www.dkfindout.com/us/more-find-out/festivals-and
-holidays/halloween/
Read more about Halloween, and watch how to make a
paper-plate mask.

Ducksters: Holidays – Halloween
https://www.ducksters.com/holidays/halloween.php
Learn fun facts about the holiday.

Index